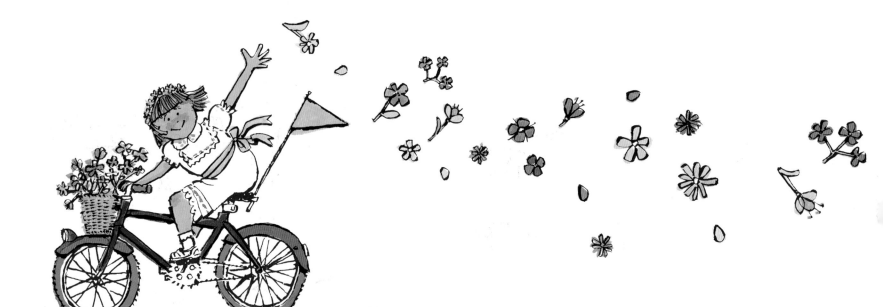

FLOWER GIRL

By KATHY FURGANG Pictures by HARLEY JESSUP

VIKING

VIKING

Published by the Penguin Group

Penguin Putnam Books for Young Readers, 345 Hudson Street, New York, New York 10014, U.S.A.

Penguin Books Ltd, 80 Strand, London WC2R ORL, England

Penguin Books Australia Ltd, Ringwood, Victoria, Australia

Penguin Books Canada Ltd, 10 Alcorn Avenue, Toronto, Ontario, Canada M4V 3B2

Penguin Books (N.Z.) Ltd, 182-190 Wairau Road, Auckland 10, New Zealand

Penguin Books Ltd, Registered Offices: Harmondsworth, Middlesex, England

First published in 2002 by Viking, a division of Penguin Putnam Books for Young Readers.

1 3 5 7 9 10 8 6 4 2

LIBRARY OF CONGRESS CATALOGING-IN-PUBLICATION DATA
Furgang, Kathy.
Flower girl / by Kathy Furgang ; illustrated by Harley Jessup.
p. cm.
Summary: Anna isn't happy when she learns that she will be a flower girl
in Aunt Julie's wedding, until she looks at wedding photographs and tries on Grandma's veil.
ISBN 0-670-88950-4 (hardcover)
[1. Weddings—Fiction.] I. Harley Jessup, ill. II. Title.
PZ7.F96635 Fl 2001 [E]—dc21 00-010965
Rev.

Printed in Hong Kong
Set in Century Expanded
Book design by Nancy Brennan

To my husband, Adam

—K.F.

To my mother and father

—H.J.

Hide-and-seek is the game we play at Grandma's house. When I hide, sometimes I listen to people talking. Today while I was hiding, I heard them talking about me!

Aunt Julie is getting married, and she wants me to be her flower girl.

My hiding place was under the couch.
Mama and Aunt Julie didn't know I was listening.
Mama told Aunt Julie that I should wear flowers
in my hair at the wedding.

I wish I could hide under the couch
until the whole wedding is over.

Mama thinks that all girls love
everything about weddings.
She'll want me to be excited
about being a flower girl.
I say there's nothing fun for
kids to do at weddings.

I would rather ride my bike
or go swimming.

Soon I was found. I needed a new place to hide. As I ran through the house I saw Grandma open the attic door. Mama and Aunt Julie followed her up the stairs.

I had never been in Grandma's attic before.

The stairs creaked with every step.
The attic was dusty and smelled like Grandpa's old beach bag.
Everything was about a hundred years old.

But it was all brand-new to me.

I crouched down behind an old rocking horse where no one could see me. Grandma opened up a big pink box and pulled out a long white gown. I stuck my hand out and touched the smoothest thing I had ever felt.

From the picture Grandma held up, I could see it had been my mama's dress.

There was a box from Grandma's wedding, too.
Her pictures were in black and white.
In the pictures Grandma looked so young and beautiful.

Grandpa was so skinny!

That's when I had to come out of
my hiding spot. "Surprise!" I yelled.
"Let me try on that veil!" Grandma let me.

When I put on the long white veil,
it touched the floor.
Everyone smiled at me,
so I knew I looked fabulous.

I even tried on silky white
gloves that went all
the way
up my
arms.
Mama put the
right finger in each
hole for me.
She said the gloves
are filled with
memories.

If I ever get married,
I'll have a cake like the
one in Grandma's picture.

It will be five layers
tall and dripping with
whipped cream.

My dress will be like Mama's, and sweep just
above the ground when I walk.

Or maybe it will be like Grandma's,
where the back drags
on the floor.

"Isn't it exciting, Anna?" Grandma asked.

"And now, you may kiss the groom!" she said dancing around the room.

What? They make you kiss a boy right there in front of everyone?

No thank you!

I pulled off the gloves.
Aunt Julie snatched them up
and put them on right away.
By now she had tried on Mama's
dress three times.

Mama and Grandma
stared and smiled.

"Anna?" my cousin yelled from down the stairs.

"Come outside! You're missing the fun!"

I looked at myself in the mirror and took off Grandma's veil.

No more wedding talk for now.

The sun was hot outside. We all
climbed the biggest tree in the yard.
From way up high I could still see
them all through the attic window.
I'll bet Aunt Julie's going to wear
Grandma's veil.

Maybe I'll wear the veil, too.
If I get married.

For now, I'll just be the flower girl.

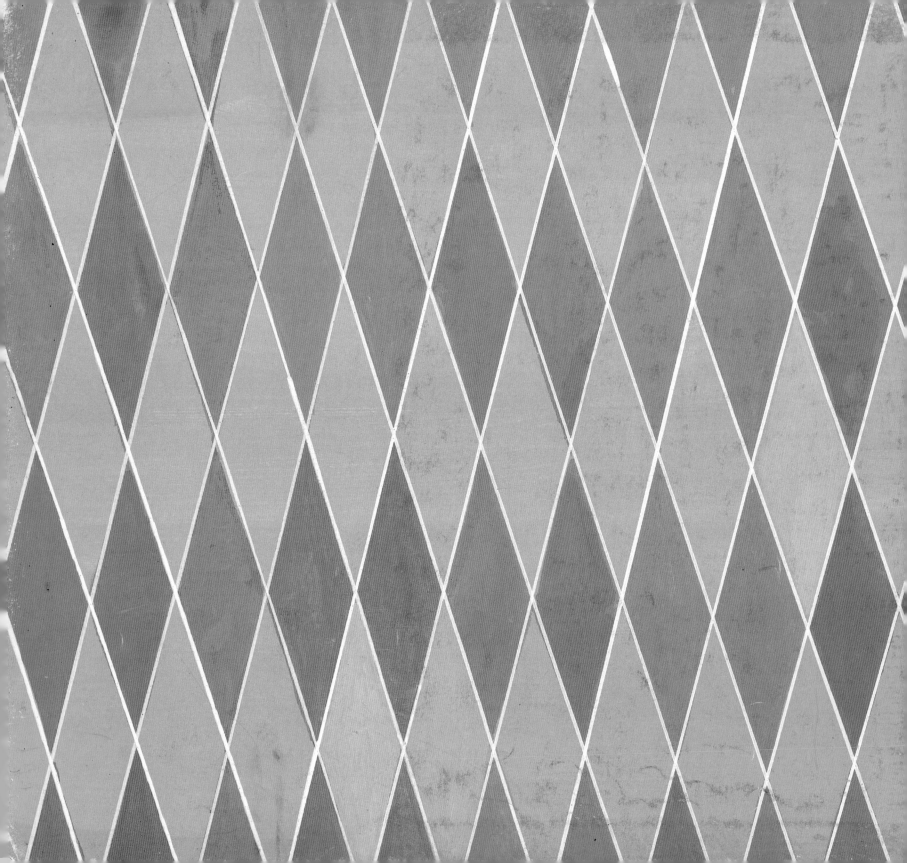